# This book belongs to:

. . . . . . . . . . . . . . . . . . . . . . . . . . . . . . . . . . . . . . . . . . . .

For Kevin - for putting up with the world's fussiest eater all these years. A.S.

To Jacob Hammond Banggiyarri Beverstock - a very brave eater! L.M.

## OXFORD
### UNIVERSITY PRESS

Great Clarendon Street, Oxford OX2 6DP
Oxford University Press is a department of the University of Oxford.
It furthers the University's objective of excellence in research, scholarship,
and education by publishing worldwide. Oxford is a registered trade mark of
Oxford University Press in the UK and in certain other countries

Text copyright © Amber Stewart 2011
Illustrations copyright © Layn Marlow 2011

The moral rights of the author and illustrator have been asserted
Database right Oxford University Press (maker)

First published as *Bramble the Brave* in 2011
This edition first published in 2018

British Library Cataloguing in Publication Data
Data available

ISBN: 978-0-19-276850-6

10 9 8 7 6 5 4 3 2 1

Printed in China

Paper used in the production of this book is a natural,
recyclable product made from wood grown in sustainable forests.
The manufacturing process conforms to the environmental
regulations of the country of origin.

# My First Milestones

# Berries are Best

## Amber Stewart · Layn Marlow

**OXFORD**
UNIVERSITY PRESS

Bramble had a nose for adventure,
and Twig was never far behind.

With Bramble leading, they would dig
their way under Buttercup Meadow,
making mole hills as big as mountains
as they went, and popping up to
play with friends.

Bramble was the burrow's bravest mole,
but she was also the burrow's fussiest mole.

Her nose for adventure
simply disappeared . . .

. . . at breakfast,
lunch and dinner.

She didn't like food
that was slimy . . .

or crunchy,
or had bits in.

Food with bits in made her tummy shudder.

One warm day, the family went pond dipping and Bramble waded fearlessly through the slippery weeds.

But when Mummy made pondweed soup,
Bramble took one small sip and said,
'I don't like it. It's slimy.'

When Daddy took them to
Lucky Tree Hill, Bramble was the
first to tumble down it hunting
for four-leaf clovers.

But when Daddy made four-leaf clover salad,
Bramble took one nibble and said,
'I don't like it. It's crunchy.'

When Bramble and Twig went adventuring
deep into Rabbit Tail Wood, Bramble
picked hazelnuts from the highest
and trickiest branches.

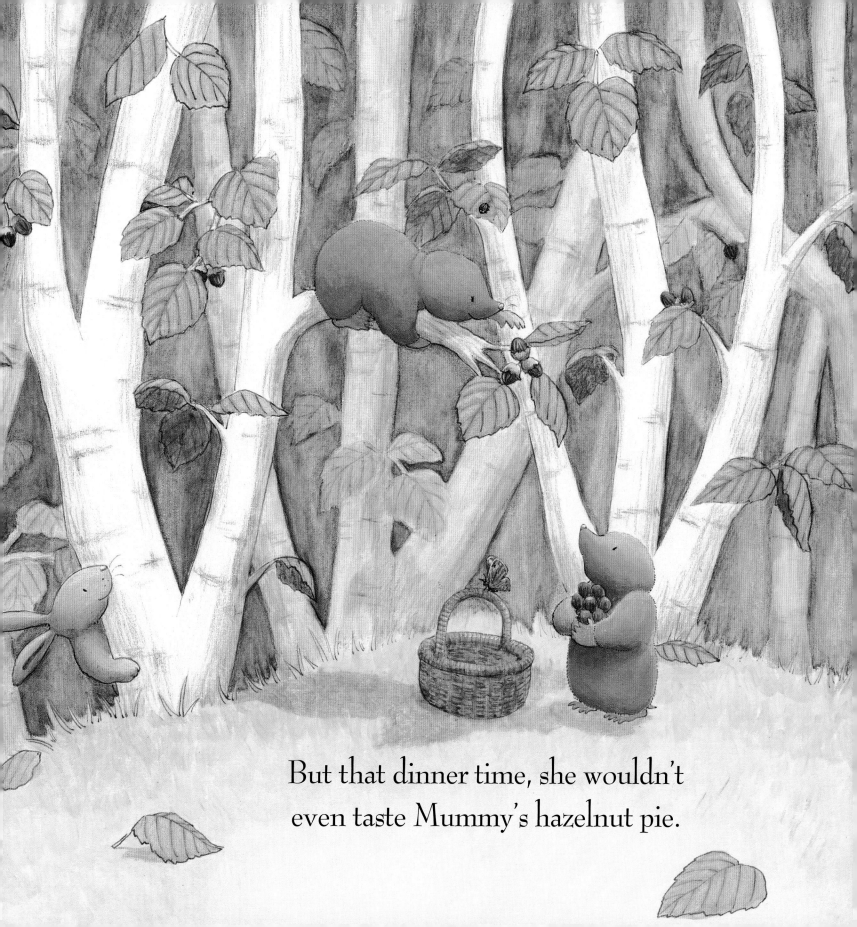

But that dinner time, she wouldn't
even taste Mummy's hazelnut pie.

'I don't like it,' she said firmly. 'It's got bits in.'
'How do you know you don't like it,' asked Twig,
through a mouthful of pie, 'if you don't try it?'

'I just know,' said Bramble.
'I know I don't like it.
I know that I only like berries.'

The more fuss was made,
the further Bramble dug
in her heels.

So for a whole week, Mummy and
Daddy turned a blind eye, and
Bramble ate nothing but berries.

She ate berries until her
paws looked splashed
with purple paint.

And her whiskers
always felt sticky.

At the end of that week . . .

. . . the bunnies came to stay for a day and a night.
With brave Bramble as their guide . . .

the five little friends dug, and hopped, and
followed their leader, for the whole afternoon.

When Mummy called two tired moles
and three droopy-eared bunnies for dinner,
Bramble looked down at her special,
separate bowl of berries.

Suddenly, Bramble wondered if it
was babyish to eat only berries?

If she could dig so deep, roll so fast,
and lead so fearlessly, was she
brave enough to eat a cress sandwich?

So Bramble took a nibble,
and said, 'I do like it.
I like crunchy!'

And then a sip
of pondweed soup,

and a big helping
of clover salad.

But everyone's favourite was Mummy's
hazelnut pie . . . bits and all.
'Yummy!' said Bramble, patting her
very full tummy.

As Mummy tucked the friends into
bed, she whispered to Bramble,

'Being brave means you try new
things . . . so you really are the
burrow's bravest little mole.'

'Berries all the time are boring,' agreed Bramble sleepily, 'especially for a mole with a nose for adventure!'

## My First Milestones
# Ten Top Tips

Here are some hints and tips for encouraging your toddler to
enjoy a varied and healthy diet, just like Bramble in this story.

**1** Offer tiny portions. A plateful of unfamiliar foods can be intimidating for little ones and small tastes keep fear at bay!

**2** Use familiar foods you know that your child likes as a base for adding variety.

**3** Make sure your toddler has an appetite when it comes to mealtimes (so avoid too much snacking in between).

**4** Talk with your toddler about the food they're eating! Describing tastes and textures really encourages children to try things.

**5** When it's warmer, how about eating outside? A change of scene can sometimes make children more adventurous!

**6** Give them control. Don't insist they eat everything you've provided — this is bound to lead to tension. Let them come to new foods when they're ready.

**7** If your child doesn't want to eat something it's not a reflection of your culinary skills — so don't take it personally!

**8** Try adding flavours to foods that otherwise might seem too bland or plain. Dipping bowls of condiments and sauces are fun for children to use with carrot sticks, for example.

**9** Remember that reluctance to try new foods is a normal part of growing up — it was probably the same for you when you were small!

**10** Don't give up — offering new tastes should always be something that's there for your toddler.